Dear ....

MERRY CHRISTMAS

With love from

....

First published in hardback in 2013 by Hodder Children's Books
This paperback edition published in 2014.

Illustration copyright © Zdenko Basic and Manuel Šumberac 2013

Carmelite House, 50 Victoria Embankment, London EC4Y 0DZ

The right of Zdenko Basic and Manuel Šumberac to be identified as the illustrators
of this Work has been asserted by them in accordance
with the Copyright, Designs and Patents Act 1988.

A catalogue record of this book is available from the British Library.

ISBN: 978 1 444 9 4234 7

Printed in China

Hodder Children's Books is a division
of Hachette Children's Books,
an Hachette UK Company

www.hachette.co.uk

The Night Before Christmas

Written by Clement C. Moore

Illustrated by Zdenko Basic and Manuel Šumberac

A division of Hachette Children's Books

'TWAS THE NIGHT BEFORE CHRISTMAS,
WHEN ALL THROUGH THE HOUSE
Not a creature was stirring, not even a mouse.
The stockings were hung by the chimney with care,
In hopes that Saint Nicholas soon would be there.

NORTH POLE
25 DEC

The children were nestled all snug in their beds,
While visions of sugarplums danced in their heads.
And Mama in her kerchief and I in my cap
Had just settled down for a long winter's nap.

When out on the lawn there arose such a clatter,
I sprang from my bed to see what was the matter.
Away to the window I flew like a flash,
Tore open the shutters and threw up the sash.

The moon on the breast of the new-fallen snow

Gave the lustre of midday to objects below,

When what to my wondering eyes should appear,

But a miniature sleigh and eight tiny reindeer,

With a little old driver so lively and quick,

I knew in a moment it must be Saint Nick!

As dry leaves that before the wild hurricane fly,
When they meet with an obstacle, mount to the sky,
So up to the housetop the coursers they flew,
With sleigh full of toys and Saint Nicholas, too.
And then, in a twinkling, I heard on the roof
The prancing and pawing of each little hoof.

He was dressed
all in fur from
his head to his foot,
And his clothes were
all tarnished with
ashes and soot.

As I drew in
my head and
was turning around,
Down the chimney
Saint Nicholas
came with a bound.

A bundle of toys he had flung on his back,
And he looked like a peddler just opening his pack.
His eyes how they twinkled! His dimples how merry!
His cheeks were like roses, his nose like a cherry!

His droll little mouth was drawn up like a bow,
And the beard on his chin was as white as the snow.
The stump of a pipe he held tight in his teeth,
And the smoke, it encircled his head like a wreath.

He had a broad face and a little round belly
That shook when he laughed like a bowl full of jelly.
He was chubby and plump, a right jolly old elf,